A Fearsome Day

by Mary Swann

A Fearsome Day

Requests for information should be addressed to

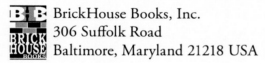 BrickHouse Books, Inc.
306 Suffolk Road
Baltimore, Maryland 21218 USA

ISBN 978-0-932616-87-6

Designed by Carmen M. Walsh
www.walshwriting.com

Distributed by Itasca Books
www.itascabooks.com

Printed in the United States of America

for Anders

For weeks Allen had been excited about his birthday...

but then something changed. His mind began to fill with upsetting thoughts.

3

His family noticed his gloomy mood.

Having no idea what was bothering him, they tried to cheer him up by talking about his birthday.

This just seemed to make everything worse.

The night before his birthday, Allen went up to bed a little early.

His mother read him a story, and he pretended to fall asleep.

After she had gone downstairs, he rolled around in his bed, listening to the coyotes in the mountains.

At last, he dozed off while their familiar voices kept his deepening dread at bay.

When morning came, Allen was four.

On this day, he had told everyone, things would be different.

He would be ready to go to the dentist. He would learn to tie his shoes. He would take his plate to the sink. He might even let himself be dropped off at his friend Jamie's house without asking his mother to come inside for a single minute.

9

Now he was afraid to get out of bed.

He didn't dare look in the mirror.
What if he was someone else?

He didn't dare put on his favorite
clothes. What if they didn't fit?

Most of all, he dreaded that
someone would come into his room
and remind him of everything he
had saved up to do.

When his mother and his brother, Sam, finally did come in, they sang "Happy Birthday" and reminded him that it was time to walk out to the bus stop with them. He mumbled that he would rather stay in bed. Sam begged him to get up.

"Hurry, Allen," he said. "I want you to open my present before I go to school!"

Allen rolled his eyes and said, "Later."

They gave up and got ready to leave without him.

"Al, sweetheart, I made you a little honey toast. I'll be right back," his mother said.

The bells on the front door jingled.

It was a long walk out to the end of the lane, and Allen stayed in his bed until they were probably almost there. He was thinking and dreading, but something kept interfering with his dread-filled thoughts.

It was the idea of a little honey toast.

15

The idea was enough to make
him slide out of bed and slither,
carefully, under all the mirrors
and windows along the way,
into the kitchen.

There it was, all brownish and rough, with a golden sheen—not cut up, which he would not have wanted—waiting for him in the middle of a dark blue plate.

He reached out, slipping his palm under the toast like a spatula.

He bit off a little corner.

As he licked his sticky mouth, he thought to himself, "It might not be so bad to change. I mean, not if I could change into something I wanted … like … a coyote."

He felt a little funny.
He still could taste the honey.
He twitched. Was he a bunny?

No, much too big! But hairy, fuzzy, and kind of bunny-colored.

What had he just been thinking? … oh, COYOTE! It was his birthday, and he was a coyote! He shook himself.

He didn't feel that different, but of course he was. It was ok, though. He just needed to get out—it was so hot in here.

21

The big coyote who was Allen was thin, terribly thin, and he slithered out through the cat door without rubbing a single grayish hair the wrong way.

Once outside, he paused for a fierce stare through the kitchen window and for a mouthful of the birdseed that was scattered along the sill.

Then away he went, into the wild world where coyotes belong. He stayed out there for a long time, not minding the change anywhere near as much as he might have expected.

Perhaps the biggest change was always feeling hungry.

There was another boy in another part of the mountains who loved wild creatures.

He was absolutely fearless and even a little wild himself. He often wished that he could be a wild animal. He also sometimes wished that he could be a dog. (This might have been easier than, say, a mountain lion or a coyote, but he hadn't seriously tried.)

The boy's name was Ansel.

One morning, Ansel and his older brother, Simon, were having breakfast together. It was the weekend, and they could take as long as they liked.

They could draw—which Simon was doing—or look out the window—which Ansel was doing—and, yes, even bicker to their hearts' content, since their parents were busy in the next room.

"I want to be the lion king," said Ansel.

"Well, I'm going to be the lion king for Halloween. You know that. Mom's making me a costume," said Simon.

"Well, Luke said I could borrow his from last year," Ansel said.

"You can't be the lion king if I'm being the lion king. I won't let you."

"But I want to … We both can, Simon. I want to, and Mom said …"

"Mom said I can, not you. You can be a knight. You can have my sword."

"No, Simon, no."

Simon threw down his colored pencil,
got up from the table, and sauntered off.
Ansel sat very still, contemplating the
notch he had carved in his honey toast.

When he looked up, he was staring into
the lightest eyes he had ever seen.

33

34

A big, furry face was watching him through the kitchen window. Its eyes held his gaze so firmly that he was speechless. He swallowed and stared back.

"Simon," he finally whispered.

"Simon, c'mere."

Simon was too annoyed to pay any attention.

"Look," Ansel whispered, "a coyote!"

He felt prickly and excited.

The coyote seemed to be looking right
into him and concentrating very hard,
as if it had something in mind.

There was a huge tug on his heart, but
Ansel was not afraid.

He picked up his toast and started
to move towards the kitchen door,
keeping his eyes on the bright, bright
eyes that were following him.

"Ansel! Wait!" rasped Simon, turning around. "Where are you going?"

Ansel didn't answer.

He heard his brother, but he had already opened the door and gone out barefoot into the cool autumn day …

… pulled irresistibly around the corner of the house until …

he stood only a few yards away from the calm coyote.

The coyote had turned its head as Ansel approached so that it was still looking directly at him …

but it now seemed most intent on what Ansel was holding in his hand.

Ansel knew exactly what to do.
He reached out his flat palm with the
honey toast balanced in the middle.

The coyote leaned forward, taking a little step, and grabbed it just like a dog taking a milkbone. He crunched the toast and slurped it down in much the same way.

His lips were glazed with honey,
His drool was extra runny.
Why did his wolfish shape look funny?

Something strange was happening.

Before the little bit of drool that Ansel had been watching hit the ground, the coyote was gone and a boy in pajamas was standing there—right in front of him.

"Ohhhh … thanks," said the boy.
"I love honey toast!"

He sniffed and cleared his throat.

A few tears were leaking out of the
corners of his eyes.

"Oh," said Ansel, amazed. "Aren't you
a coyote? I thought you were a coyote.
Aren't you? … Who are you?"

"Allen," said the boy. "I mean, I'm a kid. I'm really a kid."

He sniffled a little.

"I didn't want to change, but I had to, I guess. It wasn't that bad. It was ok, being a coyote … but I just want to be a kid—just a kid, actually."

"Cool," said Ansel. "I always think about being a dog. Sometimes I think I AM a dog! … maybe I am … I really WANT to be a dog.

Is it hard to change?"

"Yes," said Allen, lying.

It had been too easy, and he didn't want other people to start doing it.

Even though he had gone back to being a kid again, he felt different. He WAS different …

But he liked this boy. He liked him very much.

"Who are you?" he asked.

"Ansel," said the boy.

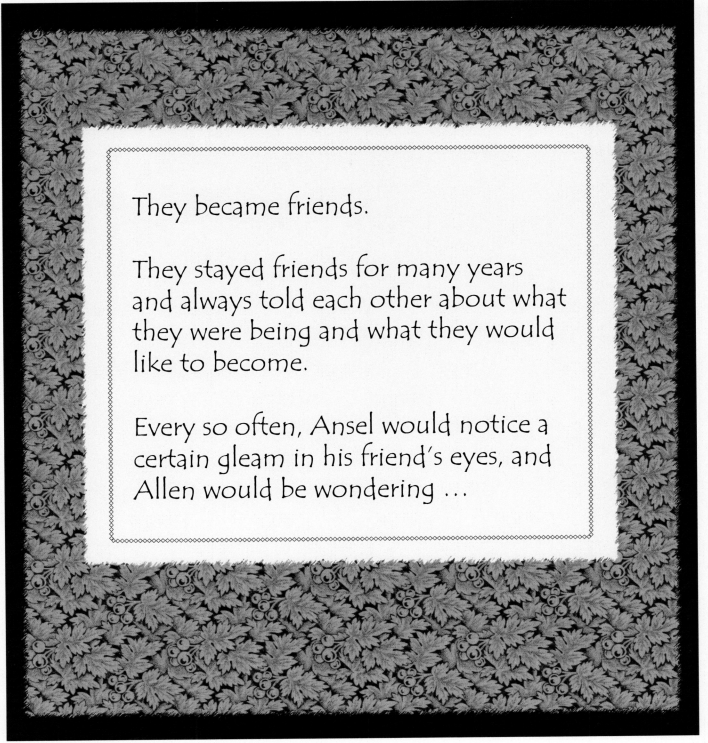

They became friends.

They stayed friends for many years and always told each other about what they were being and what they would like to become.

Every so often, Ansel would notice a certain gleam in his friend's eyes, and Allen would be wondering …

Most of the time, he had.

The End